ZERRON

Issue # 1

"POWER WITHIN"

CREATED BY
DEION TILLETT

To order additional copies of this book, contact:
Xlibris
844-714-8691
www.Xlibris.com
Orders@Xlibris.com

ISBN: 978-1-6698-1894-6 (sc)
ISBN: 978-1-6698-1893-9 (e)

Print information available on the last page

Rev. date: 03/31/2022

ZERRON

Issue # 1

"POWER WITHIN"

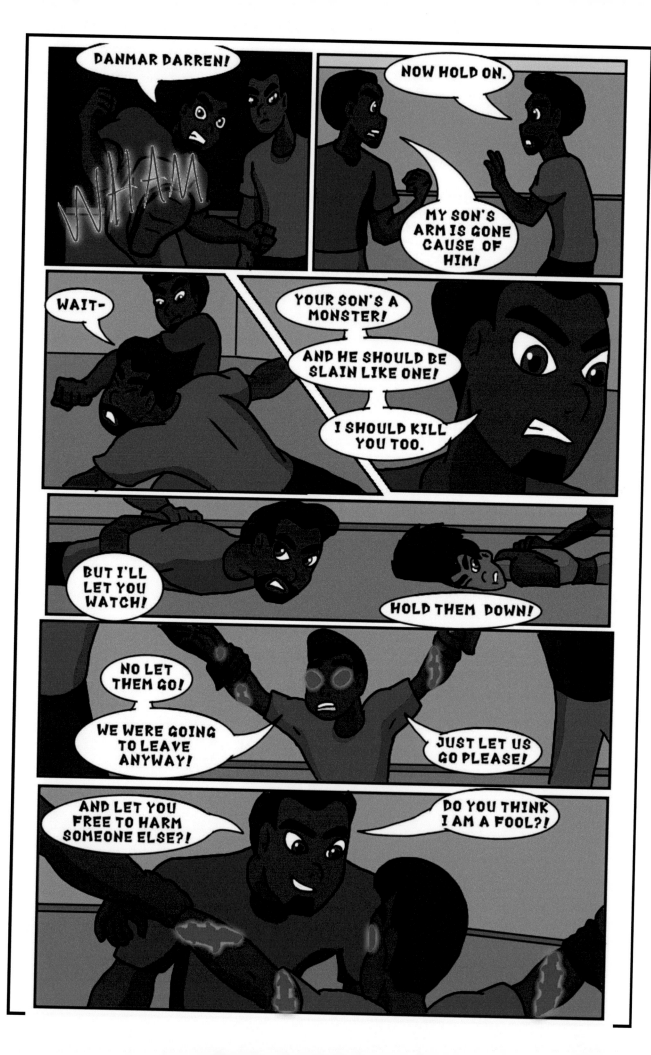

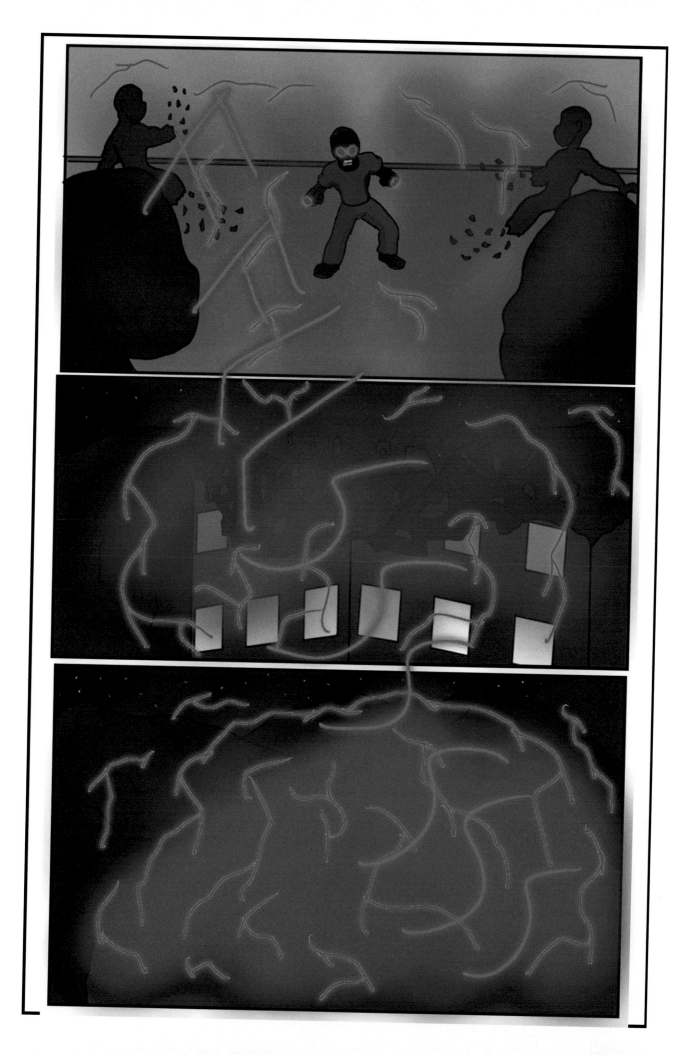

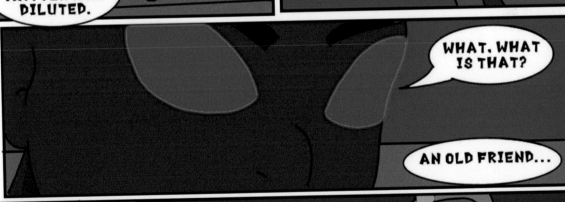

ZERRON

AQUILLO
COMICS

ISSUE #2

NEXT ISSUE :
" EXPERIMENTS"

CREATED BY
DEION TILLETT